Moonlig... ... ...

Paris

Baby Girl

Book II

In the Beginning
Moonlighting in Paris
City by the Bay
Bite the Big Apple
Caribbean Heat
Return to the Bay
Prison of the Past
Baby Girl Box Set

Elle Klass

Moonlighting in Paris

Books by Elle, Inc.
225 College Dr. #65504
Orange Park, FL 32065
Booksbyelle10@gmail.com

Author's Disclaimer

Moonlighting in Paris

Other Young Adult Books by Elle Klass

St. Augustine Novellas
Bloodseeker Series
Book 1 The Vampires Next Door
Book 2 The Monster Upstairs
Book 3 The Ghost Within

hidden journals
Isandro

Zombie Girl
Book 1 Premonition
Book 2 Infection
Book 3 Retribution

In the Beginning

*I*n the Beginning. Twelve-year-old Cleo calls a shack in Brennan, California home. She lives there with her mother who is, at best, a part-time mom. Her mother disappears, leaving Cleo to fend for herself. With no other choice she jumps on board a train to the closest city.

In the city, she meets a gang of other child vagabonds, forms close friendships with them, and an especially close bond with Einstein their leader. Together the foursome begin a thieving spree in the name of survival. It is during a heist that two of the vagabonds are caught, leaving Cleo and Einstein on the run. They continue their act across the country, finally stopping when they have enough savings to start a life together.

They choose a southern city, settle, and start their quiet life. Einstein takes a job as a dishwasher and Cleo begins a lifelong love for cooking. Their love for each other deepens by the day. They make friends with their next door neighbors, James and his daughter, LulaBell. Cleo and LulaBell become friends and through LulaBell's studies, Cleo learns about Paris. As the heat from their past crimes resurfaces with copy-cat thefts, Cleo and Einstein decide to leave for Paris.

It is on their last night in the sleepy southern city that Cleo finds her life in turmoil. In a single moment, Einstein's life is violently taken. James offers to get Cleo a passport. She accepts his offer. Her new name: Justine Holmes.

Justine

ames and LulaBell transported me to the bus station so I could hop the bus to the airport. I thanked them and we gave each other huge hugs. I watched their truck pull away and meandered into the station.

Between the second and third stops I had a six-hour gap between busses so I explored. I found a salon within a few blocks of the station and resolved to get my hair done. The name Justine Holmes demanded class, which I had little of in my present condition. The experience was new and exhilarating. As a child my mom took household scissors when my hair grew out of control.

The beautician had deep scarlet lopsided hair; it hung longer on the left side of her face than the right. I wanted something more conservative, so I asked for blond highlights throughout the top, and underneath kept my natural chocolate. She trimmed several inches off the back, shaping it with long layers. She then styled it and handed me a vanity mirror. I no longer looked like homely, abandoned, and poor distraught Cleo, but Justine.

To top off my new look I bought both a pedicure and manicure. My feet and hands were in gnarly shape. I sat in a massage chair with my feet in a tub of warm bubbling water. The mechanical fingers of the chair wrenched the kinks in my back giving me both pleasure and pain. When she finished my feet, she rushed me to a seat and dipped my fingers in warm water then clipped away my dead skin. I went with the more expensive gel polish, hoping it would last longer, and a French manicure. By the time she finished my toenails and fingernails were so eye-catching they looked as though they belonged to someone else. I looked in the mirror and saw a gorgeous young woman. For the first time in days, since Einstein's death, joy overcame me.

My physical makeover complete, I returned to the bus station and continued my journey to the airport. On the ride, I concluded my style of clothing needed a makeover too. I wore faded jeans, a T-shirt, and a heavy blue hoodie, hardly Justine glamor material. I needed dresses, skirts and fashionable sandals and boots.

At the airport I purchased my one-way ticket, which consisted of two stops - New York and Moscow, Russia - spending a grand total of thirty-three hours in flight. I had nothing but time, so I shopped, buying a couple elegant outfits before boarding. The airport wasn't any more confusing than the bus or train stations, although the security procedure was ridiculous and demeaning. I checked my bag and carried just my backpack, which I stuffed into a new, classier purse.

I hadn't flown in a plane and my stomach fluttered with anxiety. My mind envisioned an entire scenario: an unforeseen object crashing into us, causing a huge gap of twisted metal beneath our feet to open. It swallowed us and created a mass commotion among the passengers. People screamed and held onto seats or other objects to keep from being sucked into the oblivion and plummeting through the Earth's thick atmosphere to their deaths. I positioned my purse between my feet after takeoff, with a strap around my ankle in case my scenario rang true. When I plummeted to my death my pack was going with me, which I know, sounds silly, but my entire life, including important memories, were inside it.

The airline offered a meal, but it tasted disgusting, nothing like my cooking. For the price of a ticket, they should serve gourmet food. I lost my appetite. They showed a movie, but headphones cost four dollars. I took a headphone set when the man in the seat ahead of me sidetracked the flight attendant. The movie stunk, and I stuffed the headphones into the pocket sewn into the seat in front of me. Tendrils of warm fluid continued to rise and fall behind my eyes as memories of Einstein burned deep inside me.

I refocused myself and people watched. The man across from me ordered and drank seven tiny bottles of Chardonnay. A family sat kitty corner to my seat. The two older hellions bounced in their seats and down the aisles while the younger child sat quiet. The parents tried to scold the older two children, and they grew calmer, but then acted up when an opportunity arose. I sat next to a man who slept, snoring louder than the jet engine. His head, followed by his body, continued to slump onto me. I pushed him away from me, within minutes, he slumped back on me. A stocky woman barreled herself through the aisle and disappeared into the restroom just behind my seat. When she reappeared ten minutes later, so did a putrid odor, which nearly caused me to pass out. I forced my shirt over my mouth and nose, curling my face into my knees to suck in the fresh scent of my clothing.

Another person a couple rows in front of me kept talking on his phone and fiddling with his computer. Curious, I took a stroll to the restroom in front and attempted to sneak a quick glance. His coal eyes caught my look-see, and he closed the lid of his computer. Another passenger, his eyes shaking and bouncing, kept staring over his shoulder in my direction. I nicknamed him Mr. Dancy Eyes. My instincts or sixth sense kept me away from him. When the plane finally landed in Moscow, I was happy. I got off and stretched my legs even though I still had one more short flight.

I walked the entire airport during my layover stretching my cramped legs. My new identity and age made it possible for me to buy alcoholic beverages. A tall, thin man with a distinct case of male pattern baldness creeping across his head sat next to me at the bar, and asked, "Is this seat taken?"

"No."

"A beautiful lady like you traveling alone?"

My sixth sense told me to lie. "Yes, I'm meeting my fiancé in France."

His lips curled into a thin smile. "What a coincidence. I'm headed to Paris too. We have a couple hours, would you like another?"

"Thank you. So, what takes you to France?"

"We need to properly introduce ourselves. I'm Joe, and you are?" He took my hand and placed a kiss on it.

"Justine. Nice to meet you, Joe." I responded, regaining control of my hand.

"Well, Justine, it's a pleasure to meet you. I have business in Paris."

From the corner of my eye, I spotted Mr. Dancy Eyes from the plane, was it possible he was on his way to Paris too? I ignored his bouncing eyes which glared into my bare, broken hearted soul and continued my conversation with Joe accepting his drink offer. I drank slow and cautious, not wanting to get belligerent

before boarding my last flight. It so
happened Mr. Dancy Eyes was on my next
flight too.

A New World

*I*n Paris, I stepped into the fresh air and inhaled filling my lungs. Taxis and busses lined the roadways to carry people to their destinations. Without thought I boarded a bus headed towards a hotel, first checking to see if Mr. Dancy Eyes was around, I didn't see him. The bus dropped me off in front of a posh hotel, but I snuck off, not wanting a room yet. My legs needed to move after being scrunched in an airplane seat for several hours, and my belly rumbled from hunger.

I walked around Paris and took in the sights. The sun disappeared and evening settled upon the city. Paris was different to American cities I'd seen. The buildings and structures alluded they were older than time and added a mystical appeal to the city. Fewer cars littered the roads, many people walked, or rode bikes. The city was compact, opposite of American cities. I walked a few miles and stopped at a deli with outdoor seating. I opted to eat beneath the stars. Unable to read French, the waiter translated for me. My stomach betrayed my mind, I ate half the flatbread melt.

Einstein lingered in my thoughts and his caress as we first snuggled in the warehouse together. His arms holding me tight... pushing me out of the way, then his blank stare into my water filled eyes. I stood up, tears in the corners of my eyes, and threw money at the table as if it would catch the bills.

I needed a quiet place to gather my thoughts and collect myself. Not a cheap motel or abandoned building, but something grand like the hotel I first napped in after I left the shack. The name Justine commanded luxury beyond my wildest fantasies. Aimlessly, I ran smack into an extravagant, towering fairy tale palace hotel. Inside, glass chandeliers patched across the ceiling, and marble floors smoothed a path in front of me. Spinning in marvel, then floating in a slumber-like state I glided towards the counter.

With a thick French accent, the front desk man, his nametag read Jean, asked, "May I help you?"

"Yes, I need a room."

"Do you have a reservation?"

"A what?" I asked.

His eyebrows turned inward. "Reservation for a room. You must have one for us to place you."

My mind exploded. How stupid! I didn't understand reservations existed. I turned on my heels and walked towards the door without saying a word.

My ego deflated while bits and pieces of life with Einstein flashed through my head. From behind me a hand reached out and cradled my hand. A young man with light brown hair and deep brown velvety eyes stood opposite me. I met his eyes and peace washed through my soul. He explained a room was available and apologized for any inconvenience from the staff. He took my bags and helped me through the check-in process, then escorted me to a room on the fourth floor.

My eyes grew three sizes as I took in the room. The entire city twinkled in front of me through the opened curtains.

Creams, gold, and shades of red completed the décor.

He pointed towards the mini bar. "Please help yourself free of charge, it's stocked." He walked to a cabinet and opened it revealing a TV. "If you need anything ask for me, Didier. I will make sure you are taken care of." He spoke American well, but the words rolled off his tongue with an alluring French accent.

Stunned, I searched to find the words, tears pooling in the corners of my eyes. "Thank you." I mustered in a near whisper.

After he left, I checked out the rest of the room. In the bathroom a basket filled with designer lotions, bubble baths, soaps, shampoos, conditioners, and deodorants sat on the marble counter. Towels wearing the hotel emblem hung in tidy triangles from a golden bar. I squeezed my hand around a towel, its softness and thickness squished between my fingers. The stocked mini bar contained liquors, wines and snacks. Juices, sodas, various foods, and several types of cheese lined the shelves of the refrigerator. I plopped on the bed. My butt sunk into the fluffy mattress and I feared I might disappear into it. I sprawled on the bed, spread my arms and legs like a snow angel and stared at the ceiling.

My mind and body focused on my lost love. *He would have liked this place.* I took out a picture of him and ran my finger across it as if I could touch him. Then I pulled a pillow to my face and cried into its creamy softness. Tears flowed for my lost friend, lover, and family member.

I forced myself to get up and bee-lined to the mini bar, grabbed a few of the small bottles of wine, and ran a steaming hot bubble bath. The bubbles came just below my ears, and I sank into their effervescence as I drank and thought. I needed to know more about Einstein; where had he come from? Who was he? Who was Justine Holmes? That decision was mine. I needed to make an identity for her, bring her to life. My new life would be everything my other life hadn't been, and I would live in the lap of luxury. After drinking the few small bottles of wine, I grew happy and excited about my new life. I would put my past behind me. The only exception was finding more about my beloved Einstein.

After the bath I wrapped myself in a creamy-soft towel and melted underneath it. I meandered over to the mini bar again and grabbed a bottle of clear liquor with a vanilla scent. I pulled off the top and swallowed the contents of the bottle. Ewww! I chocked and gagged involuntarily. My mouth and throat were on fire, and the heat sank to my stomach, which burned. The room spun around me, and I fell against something soft.

I awoke with a pounding headache, reached for the absent covers, pried my eyes open, and attempted to focus. As my eyes adjusted, I saw a wooden table leg staring back at me, a strong hint I was lying on the plush carpet. My body didn't want to move, so I lay there staring at the ceiling. I remembered where and who I was as my eyes acclimated to my surroundings.

Through the curtains, the bright morning sun filled the sky. At the bar sat a small coffee pot, bags of coffee, and a plate of pastries. I had no memory of the pastries from the previous night. What time did I pass out? What time was it now?

I reached in my bag, and pulled out Einstein's wristwatch, it displayed seven fifteen, Friday morning. My plane arrived Wednesday evening, I settled in the room that night, now it was Friday? I remembered synching his watch to Paris

20

time upon my arrival which meant I slept over twenty-four hours. Never in my life... I let it go as caused by jet lag.

I made a pot of coffee and devoured the delicious pastries while contemplating how best to find information on Einstein. By nine thirty I headed towards the lobby, showered, dressed, and with an idea. I asked the concierge for an international paper, assuming the global news was a good starting place for my research. The concierge, Jean the same man from Wednesday, presented a paper, which I accepted. I caught the elevator back up to my room; the ride was smooth and silent.

I read and read but found nothing mentioning a hit and run in small-town Alabama, maybe the hotel had guest computers. Einstein the computer whiz taught me how to surf the net. I journeyed back to the lobby and asked Jean.

"Does the hotel have guest computers?"

"Non." He grabbed a crude map off a clear display rack and directed me to a café a few blocks from the hotel.

In the café I searched the net, looking for recent deaths, hit and runs, murders, and accidental deaths. Nothing! I typed

Alabama newspapers in the search bar. Bingo, there it was. Now I had a starting point! I looked through recent articles and found it. *Young man hit by car... driver fled scene... mysterious 911 call... thought to be driver... young woman.*

I continued reading and searching, *The young man identified as Burke Childrone...* reported *missing. His parents, owners of Childrone Publishing, flew into town to take his body... detectives worked around the clock.* My mind spun. His name was Burke, and he came from a wealthy family. Why did he leave? Did he leave of his own accord? Why else would he leave? Answers, and new questions. I continued to search for missing persons. An investigation followed his disappearance. His parents hired detectives to find their son. At one point the police suspected his parents of foul play. No evidence against them surfaced, so the police took them off the suspect list. Einstein, or Burke, disappeared into thin air. He left for school in the morning and never returned home. The police and his family presumed him dead. I knew the truth. He blended into the streets filled with runaways.

A French woman with stern eyes interrupted my research when she walked to my table and pointed towards the clock. My cue the café was closing, and I needed to leave. I gathered my notes and left. Evening settled, and a wave of brilliant lights moved across the city.

As I strolled to the hotel an overwhelming sensation that someone was following me flooded my soul, and hunger pains gripped my stomach. I attempted to reason that my new knowledge clouded my judgement, but my sixth sense told me different. A café to my right offered a place to evaluate my surroundings, regroup, and eat. It wasn't wise to continue my journey to the hotel with a spy following me. I took a seat outside and glanced over the menu, everything looked delicious. I ordered *the special*, a Parisian meat pie. It turned out to be tasty. As a homeless runaway I learned to live off the land, so to speak, meaning dumpsters, teaching me not to be picky.

I scanned the surroundings and spied a man with a bald patch on top his head standing beneath a tree a few yards from me. Mr. Dancy Eyes? Was it the same man, or my imagination going wild? His eyes bounced like a dime machine ball and he refused to look directly at me. Would someone follow me here to arrest me for my crimes? Could they arrest me on foreign soil? I didn't know the answer to any of my questions and didn't think it a coincidence he stood within eyeshot of me. Soon as I finished my meal, I threw money on the table and left.

Jumpin' Pumpkins!

I walked and walked ducking through alleys and shops attempting to confuse and lose him. When I no longer felt the sting of his bouncing eyes on my back I headed to the hotel. I spent so much mental energy evading him I'd gotten lost then I remembered the crude map Jean gave me; I unfolded it, checked street signs, and plotted the course. When I reached the hotel, I wound my way up to my room, dropped on my bed and thought of my discoveries.

Ring! Ring! The phone blasted and my body jumped in an involuntary lurch, falling off the bed. I scrambled to my feet, and picked up the phone, as if it would blow up in my hands.

"Hello?"

"Miss Holmes, this is Didier. How is your stay?" His French accent melted the words off his tongue, and my anxiety disappeared.

"I'm great, and yes, all my needs are met."

"If there is anything more I can do to make your stay unforgettable, don't hesitate to ask." Is it customary for hotel owners to call their guests?

"Thank you." I placed the phone on the receiver.

Within minutes of hanging up the phone a knock rattled the door. Room service? I hadn't placed an order. I grabbed a doll sized statue seated on a table, in case Mr. Dancy Eyes stood on the other side, and opened the door. To my thankful surprise it wasn't Mr. Dancy Eyes, but a bottle of complimentary wine and a bouquet. The delivery boys' eyes scanned the statue in my hands, and he pushed the gifts toward me as if to block my blow. With a sheepish grin I set the statue back on the table and took the vase and wine. A card on a stick hidden amongst the flowers read *Invitation*. I opened it and read, *Join me at the restaurant downstairs for dinner under the stars tomorrow, Didier* with a yes and no box underneath the print. The boy handed me a pen. I marked the yes box and gave it to him. After all, now I was glamorous Justine, and lived an exquisite life. He nodded as he caught it by the corner then scurried to the elevator.

I spent the following day shopping for glamorous Justine clothing and date material – sexy and beguiling. Stylish clothing stores littered Paris, which oddly gave me a hidden sense of security while shopping for dresses and designer shoes. My lesson for the day was understanding the difference between designer names and knockoffs. The never-ending assortment of fashions included something for everyone's taste. I bought an eye-catching green knock-off dress that my budget allowed. The front came down in a V across my chest displaying the round curves of my breasts beneath and the back fell in long, shallow layers. It was alluring and most definitely Justine.

I met Didier at the hotel restaurant as the note instructed. We ate dinner while the wine flowed. Charm surged from every word Didier spoke. His dark brown hair fell below his ears with thick waves scattering across his head, green halos surrounded his coffee-colored eyes. I'm sure he had no shortage of women chasing him and wondered what he saw in me.

I wanted to be in the present with him but my mind raced to the reason I was in Paris, Einstein. Memories of him swarmed through my mind. By contrast, his straight blond hair hung long with split ends frizzing the bottom from lack of a good haircut, most often he wore it tied back. Deep solid dark chocolate wide eyes sat the perfect distance from his nose, and his build tall and lean. Didier was at least three inches shorter with muscles exploding beneath his shirt sleeves, and a couple years older, my guess early twenties. After dinner we walked around Paris. Romance blossomed from every inch of the city blooming into vibrant flowers of passion.

Didier told life stories, and I weaved a lie about growing up in Texas. I made up the life I wished I'd lived because it would be easier to remember such a lie. About Einstein I was honest without giving more details than necessary. "My boyfriend passed away, a car wreck. That's why I'm here, it's been difficult, and I needed to get away." I dammed up the river waiting to gush behind my eyes.

The sympathy in his voice gave away his genuine concern. "We'll work on that. There is much to see here, and if you'll allow me, I will show it all to you." The breeze rustled the leaves on the surrounding trees creating music which sang to my ears – freedom and a fresh beginning.

Over the next few days we spent a lot of time together sight-seeing. The Didier tour of Paris. He adored art and took me to the Musée Picasso and Musée d'Orsay. I admired the art and the hand that painted it, however, most of it didn't make sense to me, although I didn't express that to him. Instead, I encouraged him to teach me lessons about the art.

He took me to the Eiffel Tower, Notre-Dame, and we went to Les Catacombs, tunnels and tunnels of dead people, spooky. We went to Parc Floral, one of the most stunning sights I had seen in my entire life, color and sweet aromas exploded from every angle. French people celebrated death and life and admired art and fine wine. The longer I stayed the more in love with Paris I grew. Nothing appeared real leading to the pseudo-perception that Justine was untouchable melting into the atmosphere and mystery that shrouded Paris.

After a week of wining and dining, Didier stole my breath away. He took me to a penthouse room in his hotel, blues and creams popped from the décor while silks and velvets covered the windows and furniture. The fluffy carpet squished beneath my feet, and the room was large enough it took up half the space on the top floor. Thin cream sheers held up at the corners with gold pins surrounded the bed. A massive entertainment system with items I didn't understand what they were or how to work them sat to the right of the bed. In the center of the huge room two blue velvet chaise lounges faced the entertainment center with a small table tucked between them. A two-burner stove, full size refrigerator, and breakfast bar completed the kitchenette. Long blue velvet curtains held up with gold rings covered the large picture windows puddling on the floor beneath them. A wrought iron chair was visible between the cracks in the curtains.

I padded to the curtains and pushed them aside revealing a twin wrought iron chair and small round table. The terrace extended longer than the length of the room, overlapped the next room, a small gate separated the areas. The entire city twinkled before my eyes while my mouth dropped to my feet in awe. I opened the door and took a seat allowing myself to dissolve into the breathtaking view. A few weeks ago, I couldn't have imagined being in a room this elegant, much less dating its owner.

From behind, Didier wrapped his arms around me, his mouth caressed my cheek kissing it softly, startling me. He zapped away my loneliness in that single moment, I no longer felt like a paper character in a fictional book. His gentle kisses danced across my neck, leaving a warm patch that sent tingles through my spine. I hoped this wonderful dream would last an eternity.

"How do you like the room?" He asked in his silky voice.

"It's more beautiful than any room I've ever seen."

His mouth widened into a smile. "Good, this is your room to stay in as long as you are in Paris. You don't need to worry about anything; it's all taken care of."

The poetic way he said it played a melody in my ears. The dam now opened wide, and a river of tears streamed from my eyes. Could I live here in this luxury? I was nobody, a girl who came from a small shack with no hot water! I lived on the streets and ate trash! He knew none of this, just the tale I wove - the life of Justine, not Cleo, or my alter ego before Cleo. I stood up, turned towards Didier, wrapped my arms around his neck, perched on my tiptoes, and whispered, "Thank you" in his ear. I refused to turn away such luxurious living accommodations when I had no income, and from such an exhilarating man.

He wiped the tears below my eyes. "Why do you cry?"

"Your generosity."

He folded me into his arms and kissed my lips, his tongue playing tangle games with mine. Warmth radiated through my body and the word "love" came to mind.

.

Fears and Facts

*D*idier inherited his parent's riches, their hotels, money and holdings across Europe when they passed away, making him a man of extreme wealth. He enjoyed spending time with me because I was, 'not demanding like most women, but lighthearted and always in awe of the small things in life no one else notices'.

I had little experience in philanthropy, but I wanted to feed the birds, and give money to the vagrants. This interested him. I didn't want to see people suffer in the same way as myself. I wanted them to buy a warm meal, not find a cold half eaten one in the trash. He traveled and occasionally took me with him. He taught me how to golf – a huge sport in France. I found it therapeutic to hit the little ball pretending it was Einstein's murder or a paparazzo and watch it fly.

As the woman by his side, I gained overnight unwelcomed popularity and publicity. The tabloids, newspapers, internet, and TV splashed us across their covers and headlines. My life spun without warning into an unfamiliar world I didn't understand. The paparazzi buzzed with action, the flash of their camera's blinding my eyes. They invaded our space and made private moments public. Everybody wondered who I was, *Didier's mystery woman*. He did his best to keep me out of the public eye, but the more places people saw me with him, the more popular and frightened of them I became.

The times I didn't travel with him I spent hold up in the penthouse trying to figure out the entertainment system. This amused him, someone my age, or the age he thought, who didn't understand technology. I lived as a hermit with the curtains drawn when he traveled. On occasion I pulled back the heavy drapes and sat on the terrace to read. I didn't go out much without Didier; he could handle the paparazzi, but they scared me. They lurked around corners, waiting to snap pictures. The publicity was far more than I wanted and anxiety ate a hole in my gut. What if someone recognized me? In my mind, the tabloid headlines read *Justine, thief wanted for extradition.*

He gave me a personal laptop I used to further research Einstein's disappearance and death, and our crime spree. The police hadn't linked him to the burglaries across the country, or discovered who made the 911 call the night he died. The police found Einstein's killer, and the courts prosecuted him *to the fullest extent* whatever that meant. Frank Tomey confessed to driving drunk that night and accidentally killing him. I knew better. The car aimed in my direction, Einstein pushed me, saving my life in exchange for his. The killer Frank Tomey didn't mention seeing, anyone else with Einstein. Was he that drunk? My sixth sense didn't think so. The killer was after me, not Einstein. But why? The police didn't buy his drunk story either or at least not one detective, John Young, who kept searching. Einstein's parents were wealthy and Detective Young pursued the case with vigor. He found no connection to Einstein's family, but rather a connection to another wealthy family, the Briggs. Their wealth and power became a brick wall, halting his investigation. Secrecy engulfed the family.

Charlotte Greenbrier A.K.A. Student

I used the power of the internet to find information on my mom. Not sure where to start I checked out archived newspaper articles; disappearances, strange deaths. I found many disappearances, but none my mom or even close. I looked through deaths, murders and unsolved mysteries.

Finally, I discovered a story describing a young unidentified woman found floating upstream in a river. It wasn't far from where I grew up and the date was during the time she went missing - within the months of my being alone in the cabin. The

36

article supplied a few details: female, early thirties, red hair and petite in size. The description matched my mom. Ligature marks on the women's neck suggested strangulation prior to being tossed into the river, and her attacker unknown. If this woman was my mom, did she whore herself out to the wrong man or was it a drug deal gone bad? Answers but even more questions. On a tablet beside the computer I scribbled the name of the officer in charge of the case and the author of the newspaper article. I yanked my notes off the tablet and stuffed them into my pocket.

Now I had phone calls to make, but not from my room - any calls made through the hotel were on record via the phone bill. I didn't want to be followed by Mr. Dancy Eyes, or anyone else. In the past I melted into a crowd, seen but not seen. Now each direction I turned my face stared back at me, and I longed to blend. Didier had clothes in my room, so I rummaged through them until I found something that looked acceptable. A pair of baggy pants and a buttoned shirt. I pulled my hoodie over it, rolled my hair into a cap, and took a quick glance in the mirror. Not too horrible since oversized clothes were in style.

On the streets, I needed a phone, an untraceable one... a throwaway cell phone. A jiffy store stood a few blocks from the hotel. A place selling cigarettes, candy and other miscellaneous items including disposable cell phones. I purchased one and headed to the hotel. No good. My sense of anonymity forced the need to find someplace with no connection to my present life. I spotted a small café with seating outside and nobody else around, I made my phone calls. I wasn't sure who to talk to first, but thought the nosy media might be my best choice.

The reporter who worked my mother's case was as good a place as any to start, I thought. Her office gave me a run around and after several minutes patched me through to her.

"Gina Brandt." Her voice suggested a person straight and to the point.

"Thanks for speaking with me. My name is Charlotte Greenbrier. I'm a journalism student and I would like to ask you questions about a case you worked. I have to write a paper on an unsolved mystery."

"Which case?"

"A couple years ago, the police found a woman in her early thirties with red hair floating upstream in a river?"

"Yeah, bad postmortem bruising, most likely caused by the stream's current dragging and bouncing her off the rocks. Her body decomposing for months. She didn't have ID, and no dental records or finger prints matched hers in the system." Gina Brandt's words showed no emotion.

The article ran in several papers within the area, providing no new leads. She was a mystery woman, whom nobody claimed. The tears welled up in my eyes, and my throat burned. I struggled to hold back my sorrow. My mom was a junkie and not much of a mother, but she was all I had until an unknown assailant took her from me.

"Could you describe her?" I asked.

"Sure. Caucasian, approximately five feet tall, thin, with freckles, and track marks ran up and down her arms, but the papers printed that. I was in your shoes once so I'll give you something the papers didn't print and lead nowhere, you might can do something with it. The police found a damaged picture tucked into her shoe. The extensive damage made the picture near impossible to tell the child's features or sex, except it was a picture of a child - the consensus female."

I thanked her, and she relayed which police station held the picture in evidence, in case I wanted to take a look. After hanging up I composed myself. My mother was a loser, but she hadn't left me on purpose. Someone took her from me and she loved me enough to keep my picture with her.

I paid my bill and walked. My mind needed the opportunity to mull over the new information. What involvements did my mother have that got her killed? Drugs? I knew it was drugs, well, possibly not. We lived a quiet, secluded life. Was she running from something, like I ran? Was my life a mirror of hers? Did she get pregnant with me, with nowhere to go and no one to turn to, she turned inside herself. The times she disappeared she spent days, sometimes weeks gone. I assumed she worked because she came back with money, food, and clothing. Whore with a conscience came to mind, who wanted to keep her child from following in her footsteps. Not that we had much of a life but she spent most of her time with me during my earliest years when I couldn't fend for myself.

If I called the police now, what would I ask them? So much to think over I went to the hotel, snuck up to my room without being noticed, I thought.

I sank into the tub with a bottle of wine and blasted the jets.

Didier woke me with a gentle kiss and nudge. "Justine, this is a bad habit, you... the tub and wine." His gentle voice edged towards scolding. He helped me out of the tub wrapped me in a towel, and pat dried my body. Small streams of water from the edges of my hair traced a path down my back. He placed one hand under my legs and the other across my back, lifted me up, and lay me on the bed. His kisses smothered my body sending a quake of hot shivers through me. We made sweet love. Spent, I soon slipped into sleep.

My sleep haunted me. First, in the darkened woods by my childhood shack home I, as Justine, ran from a man whom I have never seen or met. I wore nothing but shorts and a tank while deformed branches scraped against my skin as my body brushed against the trees. The man had straight black hair and coal eyes. In his hand he carried a noose. My foot got stuck between two rocks. I fell forward from the momentum of running. The leaves caught me. I twisted my head to glance over my shoulder, he vanished, and I was twelve years old and alone in the shack. In my next dream I saw my mom in a restaurant, holding a picture in her hand, arguing with the man who chased me. He handed her an envelope and left, angry. My sleep offered me no rest. I woke up confused about who I was and where I came from and a lump in my gut hinting my life was in danger. Was my mom really my mom? Deep down I knew she wasn't - we didn't look alike.

Who's Slug?

*D*idier kept me busy the next few days while I continued assessing, and determining, what my next move should be. Call the police? What would I say to them? That's when it hit me like a ton of bricks! My mother's letters! I stuffed them into my backpack when I left the shack, but I couldn't get to them until Didier left again. He commented on my strange behavior, calling it, 'melancholy'. I did my best to act appropriately. I didn't want him to suspect anything while I waited for him to have an of town emergency needing immediate attention. Each day my anxiety grew. It became more difficult to control my flailing emotions. Finally! I caught him packing. Without sounding too apprehensive leading him to think I didn't care or my restlessness had to do with him I curbed my enthusiasm.

"You're leaving?"

"Yes, I'm sorry. I will overnight at the most." His intense eyes searching my soul. I wasn't sure if the intensity was him not wanting to leave or his worry for me and my strange behavior.

To squelch his concern for me and get attention before he left I strode to his side, wrapped my arms around him, and buried my head into his chest. I wanted him to leave knowing I'd be OK. His scent and firm arms were inviting. "You go, take care of your business. You'll be gone just long enough for me to miss you." I said in my coyest playful voice.

"I do miss every moment without you." He gave me a kiss that played across my lips and lingered.

From the terrace I watched him leave. As soon as his car departed, I ran back into my room, pulled my backpack out of hiding, and tore through it, looking for the letters. I found them in the bottom, squished and bent, but present. There were four, three from someone who called himself Slug, dated three years apart. *Who would want to be called Slug?*

The first letter I was three, it read, *The Tomato Shack at 3:30 on 3/11,* the next *The Tomato Shack at 5:00 on 8/30.* I made a mental note to find out what the Tomato Shack was. Slug couldn't be his real name, so maybe Tomato Shack and Slug were code words. The next letter read, *1523 Tanwood Dr. at 2:00 on 1/20 and bring the girl.* I must be the girl, but why would someone who calls himself Slug want anything to do with me? Bells and whistles blasted in my head. My mother kidnapped me! They read like ransom letters. *Bring the girl,* the words jumped off the page at me. My suspicions of my mother not being my biological mother now confirmed. She kidnapped me! The last letter from Slug read, *this will be the last meeting. I don't want to see pictures of the child and if you refuse to bring her I will hunt you down and kill you both!!!!! Tomato Shack 10:00 4/23.* Five exclamation points, one would have been enough to make his point! His harsh words sent chills climbing up my spine. The date on the letter a couple weeks before my mother's, or kidnapper's, disappearance.

A chill swirled in the air surrounding me and it fell quiet. He killed her and now he's hunting me? Could Slug be Einstein's killer? No, Einstein's killer confessed and was sitting in jail. My mind reeled, and thoughts played through my head. Was I abducted at a young age to protect me from Slug or did my true family hire him to find me?

My mom wrote the final letter. It stated *Sweet Baby* on the envelope. I opened the letter carefully and pulled out its contents. Inside contained pictures of me dressed up in taffeta and velvet dresses, and patent leather shoes. The dates printed on the backs coincided with Slug's letter – every three years. I remembered having the pictures taken, her dressing me up, and putting rollers in my straight hair the night before taking me to the studio. The pictures were deceiving a person looking at them wouldn't know the tormented life I lived, how she abandoned me periodically for weeks at a time. Later forced to run away and live on the streets.

My heart pounded hard, and I attempted to catch my breath as I placed the pictures back into the envelope and uncurled my mother's letter...

Sweet Baby,

I know I haven't been much of a mother to ya. I haven't given ya much of a life. Without me ya wouldn't have had no life at all. I took ya and was saposed to give ya to somebody. I could't stand to see yar life end before it began. So I didn't give ya to them. I kep ya. I have always kep ya secret. Nobody

nows where ya are. The people that want ya
are powerfu. They are real rich and can do
most anything they want. I tell ya this cause
I want ya to be careful. Don't ever let them
find ya. They won't hestate to kill ya. I don't
think I'll be comin back. I do love ya and
hope ya unerstand I had to keep ya hidden
to keep ya alive.
   Mommy

My brain couldn't digest the
information put on its plate. The room
whirled out of control before my eyes.
According to my mom, she abducted me to
protect me from my true family? Who was
my family, the mafia? Why would they want
an innocent baby gone? My life just got a
hundred times more insane than a few
moments ago before reading the letters.
   My mom wasn't much of a mom. In
fact, she was a horrible mom, but she kept
me hidden, alive. I had to do something for
her so I picked up my throw away phone
and called the police. An Officer La Tige was
in charge of my mother's case. The
receptionist said he no longer worked for
them, but she would patch me through to
his partner, Officer Han. I anonymously
referred to the case and told him the

shack's location and mentioned she didn't live alone. She lived with her daughter. I hung up and dropped the phone in a sink loaded with bleach.

Next, I took the phone and smashed it with a hammer I picked up while dumpster diving in my previous street urchin life. I grabbed a small plastic garbage bag and picked up the pieces, pulled my hat over my head, and placed my sunglasses on my face. Ready with sneakers, baggy jeans, a sweatshirt and no makeup, I left. I walked to the metro station, got on and rode, where to didn't matter. A safe distance from the hotel, I got off the train and walked, dumped phone bits and pieces into the trash, then strolled back to the metro. I got off again, deposited the bag holding the rest of the phone, and then journeyed home. This woman, my kidnapper mother at least would have a grave with a marker. Good luck trying to trace me.

Aruba

 made the choice to put my past behind me. My brain reached maximum absorption and needed time to process. Justine's increasing popularity gave me a false sense of security. After all, there would be more unwanted publicity for the murderer now than during my street urchin days. Many magazines and tabloids had my, Justine's, face plastered on their front covers. Agents called me to participate in photo shoots. I accepted and fooled myself into believing the more famous I became, the less chance anyone had to kill me. Didier flipped the last time he left me alone because he couldn't get hold of me. Now he kept me glued to his side or with the bodyguard he hired for me, Sam. Sam was tall and built like a truck. Didier cared for me and worried. He wanted me safe at any cost.

A popular sports magazine approached me about doing a swimsuit photo op in Aruba. Intrigued, I accepted their offer.

Didier passed on accompanying me - the downside of running an empire - but I had Sam.

When we stepped out of the airport, the sun instantly warmed my skin and mild breezes teased my hair. A limo waited to drive us to the resort. There were twelve models, one for each month, most professionals. From feet to top of head, I stood five two and a half, a midget beside them. Gorgeous didn't describe each woman's magnificence. The tabloids and now semi-professional modeling career forced me to look at myself in a different light and accept my own beauty. True, I lacked the height, but according to a popular tabloid my *exotic looks can't be rivaled*.

The magazine set us up in a beach resort. My suite was smaller and simpler than what I had grown accustomed too. Tired from the flight and with a few hours to settle-in before our dinner, I wandered to the beach. The clear ocean water offered an unobstructed view of the tiny fish swimming below its surface. Where the ocean met the beach the tide followed a zigzag pattern. I followed the pattern for a mile or more before settling in the sand and allowing the water to move up and down my legs in a rhythmic fashion. Past moments flickered through my head - how my life had changed in a couple short years. Instead of warehouses and leftovers I flew to fascinating romantic places. As I lay my head back in the sand and closed my eyes, Einstein's face flashed behind my lids and I sensed him. I knew the moment would only last for a few short seconds so I held on as long as possible until the moment passed.

After dinner, in the quiet of my room which I shared with another model, Kamisha, and with Sam across the hall, we opened the door, allowing the breeze and calming sound of the tide to lull us to sleep. My mind was at peace, no haunted images invaded my dreams.

I woke up to Kamisha shuffling through her make-up bag. She was tall with legs that stretched forever, a figure displaying curves in the right places and skin darker than my own. I didn't feel my figure and face stacked up to hers. "Good morning," I yawned out, stretching my body.

"Good morning to you, our breakfast is on its way."

"Thanks."

"I didn't order, compliments of our employers. While working we eat what they feed us. You're new at this, huh?"

"Is it that obvious?"

Laughing, she said, "Yeah. You'll get used to it. We get a couple free days on the back, we could grab drinks and go snorkeling?"

I propped my limp body on the edge of the bed. "Yeah, I would love to have fun while I'm here."

After day two I was ready for real food, but I held fast and followed their diet and schedule. One more day and I could enjoy my surroundings, which already won over my heart. My stomach woke me up that night, rumbling like thunder. As my eyes adjusted to the darkness, from the corner of my eye a shadow passed. When I turned my head I saw nothing, and my eyes drifted to Kamisha resting in her bed. I assumed my imagination, or perhaps my hunger, was playing brain tricks. Within minutes I drifted back to sleep and woke up late. I rushed to prepare for the day.

The final day was upon me! As much as I enjoyed the experience I couldn't wait for the day to end. Scheduled tonight was a giant celebration with the girls, magazine reps, photographers, and everyone else involved.

Back in the room I checked my phone. One missed call from Didier. I looked towards my dresser to glimpse his picture I laid there on night one, but it wasn't there. Anxiously, I tossed the drawers, my suitcase and crawled under my bed. Kamisha walked into the room. "What are you doing under the bed?" She giggled, curiosity on her face.

With my butt in the air, I twisted my head, the bedspread draped over my face, my eyes peering out from under it. "I misplaced a picture of my boyfriend, Didier. It was on my dresser. Have you seen it?"

"No, but I'll help you search." Both of us tore the room apart, and both came up empty handed. "Possibly it fell and the cleaning lady accidentally threw it out."

I heaved a sigh. "Maybe." No time to ponder. I returned Didier's call and talked to him while I relaxed on the balcony for several minutes before hanging up and prepared for the night ahead.

At the after party drinks and food flowed heavily, and my eyes grew bigger than my stomach as I never starved myself on purpose. I ate, drank, and after a couple hours qualified for tipsy and having an awesome time. "You see that girl, the short blond one standing beside the food table?" Kamisha asked me.

"What about her?"

"Have you seen her the past few days?"

"Don't think so."

"It's odd, everyone else here I recognize - except her."

The alcohol kicked in and I felt no pain, so I sauntered over to her. "Hi, I'm Justine. I haven't seen you yet. Who are you with?"

Disgust twisted across her face and her eyes narrowed into slits. "I manage the catering company."

I sensed a strong bout of sarcasm and didn't like her tone, something inside me clicked, as though she thought me beneath her, so I handed her my empty glass and hissed, "That's great! I sure need a refill, you mind?"

Her slitted eyes narrowed more beneath her straight eyebrows and her lips curled into a fake smile. "Sure." A few minutes later she appeared with a new drink which she handed me.

"Thank you so much." The drippy sweetness drizzled off my tongue like cinnamon roll icing. Kamisha giggled at me from across the room. Just then a gentleman approached me, a photographer attempting small talk. I handed him the drink and excused myself to the restroom. I didn't want the drink; my sixth sense told me she was bad news.

You Don't Belong

*T*he next day Kamisha, I and a couple other girls, Ashley and Sharl, set out to snorkel then relax on the beach. Joy and importance bubbled inside as I never in my life had a *girl day*. We wiggled our toes in the sand, passed sunscreen to each other, complemented one another's bathing attire, and guy watched.

A sizzling hunk, his muscles carved from the hardest stone, and sun-kissed blond coursing through his shoulder length chestnut hair, introduced himself along with his buff friends - each one sported muscles on their muscles. They were participating in a weightlifting competition, although my mind never heard the rest as the curvature of their arms, legs, and their entire packages enthralled me. Their suits left little to the imagination. It took effort to keep the drool inside my mouth instead of pooling in the sand beneath me.

I caught the tail end of the conversation as the one with the largest bulge protruding from under his Speedo asked, "Around eight tonight at the... " His voice trailed off as his brown come get-me-eyes met my bewildered gaze. The group of male demi gods sauntered off, but Protruding Speedo's eyes, continued to linger on mine as he trailed away.

"OMG, they were hot!" said Ashley, her face covered in pure lust.

"Hot, honey." Sharl air fanned herself. "They were flawless and I'm gonna have me one later!" Hunger dripped from every pore in her body.

I scrunched my face in embarrassment. "Did Mr. Bulging Speedo..." They burst out in laughter, Ashley rolled in the sand resembling a powdered donut formed from a well-built female shaped cookie cutter. I hadn't meant to say it, the words transported from my head and out my mouth.

"I... I... " I dropped to the sand joining Ashley in a fit of laughter.

Sharl and Kamisha roared in laughter and rolled in the sand beside us, soon each of us resembled Ashley. I loved Paris but felt at home hanging with these girls in the Caribbean.

Early evening we moseyed to our rooms. Potted tropical plants positioned between puffy couches and chairs filled the lobby. An unfamiliar voice called my name. "Justine?" I scanned the lobby to find the body the voice belonged to. A resort staff member walked towards me. "This was left at the counter for you." She placed an envelope labeled *Justine* in my hand.

"Thanks." I assumed it was a message from Didier and placed it on the dresser for after my shower.

Clean and eager to see what he left me, I tore into the envelope and unfolded a note. Something fell out and hit the floor, my picture, the lost or stolen one. In red smudged lipstick the note read *You don't belong.*

My heart beat fast while my mind put the clues together. The night before my picture disappeared, I thought I saw a shadow. Old fear and memories surfaced into my conscious. Slug wanted me dead, Frank Tomey killed Einstein as he risked his life to save mine, pushing me out of the way. I clutched the letter in my hand and jetted across the hall, knocking on Sam's door. He answered immediately; my distress visible to him.

"Justine, what's wrong?" Speechless, I handed him the note. His eyes scanned it, then he shoved me into his room, entered the hallway closing the door behind him, after several minutes reappeared. "The hallway is clear, but you aren't staying in that room. You will stay here in mine." Sam called the front desk and Didier.

I planted myself on the chaise to wait him out. He paced across the room and onto balcony several times pulling at his chin and right ear while he spoke. He put up with tons for my sake. When he finished making calls I asked, "Can we get a drink?"

His eyebrows turned downward into a V. "A drink?"

"Yup, my treat. You are always there behind the scenes and I don't know you."

"A drink? Sure, sounds good."

He agreed without the hesitation I expected. Perhaps my idea hit the spot, or he was doing his job, keeping tabs on me. We headed downstairs to a bar.

I plopped my bootie on a bar stool, Sam scanned the room before taking the stool beside mine. I ordered an Aruba Ariba for myself and a beer for Sam. "How did you get into this whole body guard thing?"

"You get right to the point, don't you?" His square jaw barely moved when he spoke. "I played professional football back in the states until I injured my knee and got cut from the team. I realized maybe pro ball wasn't for me."

"Football. I've never watched." With my unfortunate upbringing, football and other spectator sports were something still undiscovered.

"Have you noticed anything odd since you've been here?"

"I might have seen someone in my room the other night and the next day a picture of Didier I brought, disappeared."

"My job is to protect you and you failed to mention this?" His voice became hard.

"I didn't think anything about it... then." I lied a little, but suspicions laced my life.

"It's probably nothing, you've become popular, threats are part of the territory, but I refuse to take this lightly." He lifted his beer and took a large swallow. "Didier is on his way here. He planned on making this a surprise but under the circumstances, you should know. You will stay with me until his arrival."

I sucked down my drink so quick the effects of the 151 Rum showed. "He is a wonderful man." I yacked on describing my first night in Paris and how Didier and I met. "Did you meet him when he hired you to protect me?"

"No, we've been friends for years. We met when I played ball. When the team cut me he offered for me to come to Paris and work for him. I needed a change and accepted his offer."

"As a bodyguard."

He chuckled. "No, not at first, I have a bachelor's in law enforcement and criminology. Didier hired me as head of security. It wasn't until you came along that he asked me to be your bodyguard."

"That seems like a demotion?"

"No, I have never seen him taken by anyone as much as he is with you. He gave me a raise to keep an eye on you and knows of your adventures wearing his clothes as a disguise."

"You got me on that one. Who ratted, Jean the concierge?"

"It doesn't matter, he worries and you are a bit of a mystery."

"Mystery, how?" I finished the last drop of my drink and ordered another.

"You show up out of the blue and ask how? What matters is he loves and cares for you; your safety means everything to him. Drink up and go nowhere." He got up and left.

Sam returned thirty minutes later. I passed the point of tipsy and reached full inebriation. I remember Sam saying, "Time to get you to bed."

The smell of coffee and Sam's voice woke me. In my half-awake mode Sam's voice reminded me of a dog barking, but as my mind adjusted to being awake, I heard him clearly. "It was a photographer... a heart attack, but after her threat, I'm not so sure... She knows, when she wakes up we'll collect everything... we'll be ready."

I pretended to be on the verge of waking up as he entered the room from the balcony, noting my stretches he offered coffee. I sat up in bed and accepted his offer, my mind sifting through his words, attempting to make sense of them. He had been right, I was calm yesterday considering a misguided soul who referred to himself as Slug wanted me dead. His written words *I will hunt you down and kill you both* flashed across my brain. A jealous girl couldn't be worse. The fact the psycho woman had been in my room made my skin crawl. I assumed it was a girl because the lipstick made the threat appear feminine.

Proposal on the Atlantic

*D*idier's yacht became visible when the sun leveled with the ocean's horizon. Reds and oranges played with the wave crests until they disappeared. The yacht docked, and I ran to him, wrapped my arms around him as we locked in a long sensuous kiss. "You're good?" He asked while he lifted me off the ground and twirled me in circles. His biceps swelled beneath his shirt sleeves threatening to rip the seams.

My feet and legs flailed in the air and one of my flip-flops flew off and sailed across the sand. The wind whipped my ponytail across my face. I brushed my hair back and our eyes met. The green part of his eyes more vibrant in the Caribbean sun. "I am. Even better because you're here." He was my knight in shining armor, my fairy tale prince.

Once we settled on the yacht, he and Sam excused themselves behind closed doors. I knew I was the topic of their conversation and my anger rose. *Why couldn't they talk about me to my face?* My past I kept secret from them - how I survived on my own without men, no bodyguard, no monetary resources, just me and my precious Einstein. We learned to survive currents of fury together.

Twenty three minutes later they reappeared. With my stern face on, I gave them each a piece of my mind. "Gentlemen if you are going to talk about me when I'm present you need to include me in the conversation. Sam, I want you to teach me self-defense in case I'm ever in a jam and neither of you," crunching my eyes into slits, I scanned each, "is present to rescue me." My ulterior motive to learning self-defense was to defend myself against the likes of Slug and whatever evil came my way. I told neither of them that tidbit of information. I focused my attention back to Didier and Sam as they swapped glances back and forth. Obviously, there was a secret going on between them that involved me; I deserved to be informed!

"You are right, our discussions involving you should include you." Didier said with a half bow, one hand behind his back.

Sam responded, "Justine, self-defense is excellent thinking, especially after yesterday's incident. We'll start as soon as we get home." Sam excused himself, leaving Didier and I alone.

Didier grabbed a bottle of wine and two glasses, gesturing for me to sit with him. "Tell me about the last few days. Did you enjoy your time?" I had to give it to him, he had a calm way of diffusing a situation. At the moment I was content to sit and talk along with a few other things... instead of argue.

We took a leisurely trek across the Atlantic and through the Mediterranean to get home to France. The final night may hold as the most romantic of my life. He bought me a special dress to wear. It was white with small silver sparkles embedded in the delicate fabric, and the neckline plunged across my breasts, leaving the crests open to viewing, it continued its flow across my arms and back, which formed into layers towards the hemline flowing longer than the front. For the finale, I put my hair up in a beehive with my long layered bangs crossing from the top of the hive and sweeping across my forehead. I completed my attire with a fragile silver chain carrying a single diamond which rested fashionably above my cleavage.

I joined Didier on the deck for a candlelight dinner, his face lit up when I came into full view. "You are an angel." He pulled out my chair and kissed the nape of my neck as I sat. After dinner, he walked to my left side and placed his hand, palm facing out in front of me, and I placed my palm down in his. He slipped a delicate white gold ring, studded with small diamonds, a single tasteful diamond in the center onto my third finger. My eyes looked into his, tears staining my cheeks as he asked, "Justine, will you marry me?" In the heat of the unforgettable moment I remembered Didier and Sam's private conversation. Now I understood why it was private.

My throat choked and tears formed in the corners of my eyes. I whispered, "Yes." We joined in a long kiss. My fears and terrors of the past floated away.

Spiked Punch

*D*espite his intimidating size, Sam was an awesome guy. We spent a couple hours in the hotel's gym daily, where he taught me self-defense moves. I could now not only squish any man in the groin or gouge an attacker's eyes out, but in one quick movement I could toss an attacker over my body and onto the floor on his back. He taught me how to shoot a gun since I asked to learn. I didn't want one but felt it would be a useful skill to have. I learned to use a knife and the location of the most debilitating area on the human body.

Sam's words I overheard the last day in Aruba played like a broken record in my mind, *It was a photographer... a heart attack, but after her threat, I'm not so sure.* As he demonstrated how to karate chop someone's neck I asked, "Was I the only person threatened in Aruba?"

"To my knowledge, yes. Concentrate." I left it alone and researched on my own, but

68

what I discovered forced disappointment to well up inside me. Protection was one thing, but keeping danger covert was just plain wrong and I knew something Didier and Sam didn't because of their secrecy. It was meeting time with both of them to gather and compare our notes.

The boys, Didier and Sam wore the guilty puppy I-left-a-present-on-the-floor expression. "Gentlemen, I understand you are concerned with my safety, but so am I. You have withheld information from me. A photographer died, seemingly of a heart attack, except he had no history of heart problems. He was the man I handed my drink to after requesting it from a rude caterer. I chose not to drink it, handing it to him and excusing myself." I gave them both the evil eye.

"My job is to safeguard your very being. I cannot do that unless you tell me everything." Sam stated with a hint of sarcasm.

"People are rude. That doesn't automatically mean they're harmful. I am as much to blame. I believe someone spiked the drink and unaware, he drank it, causing an induced heart attack."

Didier's soft eyes converged with mine and he cut in, "You believe the drink was for you?"

"Yes."

He folded me into his arms. "Sam, you remember this woman?"

"I do and I'm on it."

As Sam looked into the incident further, Didier and I planned an engagement party. He spared no expense. Over the past year and a half Didier spoiled me more rotten than sour milk. He bought me an unbelievable jewelry collection. Many of my pieces were one of a kind tailored for me. I enjoyed the jewelry but didn't live for it. I wondered if the people I stole jewelry from to pawn had missed theirs. Did I steal one of a kinds or heirlooms passed from one generation to the next? I wished they understood they helped two young children in this horrible, cruel and unforgiving world. Somehow, one day, they would understand. I would sell my jewelry to help those on the streets. In fact, most of the money I made since coming to Paris I donated. I kept a small nest egg, in case of an emergency. I didn't need it; Didier provided everything I might need and much, much more. My closet overflowed with clothes, every piece boasted a designer's name. In my opinion, clothes were clothes. They covered my body. Shoes were shoes. They covered my feet. The more I didn't fawn over my gifts the more gifts I received. He fawned on my selflessness. I told him I would be happy if he donated the money to families in need and sometimes he did.

Here and Gone

*O*ur engagement party stood out as the soirée of all soirées: co-workers, friends, and I invited Kamisha. I unexpectedly grew used to the flamboyant lifestyle, but on the inside - it wasn't me. The focus of the night centered on Didier and I and it overwhelmed me. People I barely knew, or never met congratulated me, and young ladies eyed me with envy. Whispers circulated the room: *Who is she? Where did she come from?* Then *You don't belong... You don't belong* in smudged lipstick echoed inside me. I snuck away finding a deserted room I closed the door behind me and took a deep breath then composed myself. The echoes in my head faded, and I emerged into the hallway.

The door closed behind me and a warm, sweaty hand slipped across my mouth. Heavy breathing followed by a crackling voice said, "You need to go back to wherever you came from, Justine." Her voice reverberated inside me and Sam's self-defense skills blossomed into action as I grabbed hold of the mystery woman's arm and slung her over my shoulder. A puff of dark hair and a small frame came thundering forward, landing on the floor with a loud thud. I drove my shoe into her side for good measure and ran down the hall, rounding the corner I ran into Sam.

The expression on my face gave away my fear. "Wow! Where have you been? What happened?"

"I threw her in the hall, on the floor." I squeaked. He burst down the hall.

Didier's forehead creased with lines and his eyes grew dark as he walked towards me. He scrutinized our actions. "Where is Sam?"

"I used the skills he taught me. A woman caught me from behind, I flipped her, and left her in the hall crumpled on the floor."

A look I didn't expect came over his face as his lips curled into a smile of satisfaction. "I will remember not to get on your bad side. Was she the same woman from Aruba?"

"I don't think so. Her hair was dark and short, although her size and frame are correct. With her hair covering her face, I can't be sure."

The woman disappeared by the time Sam arrived. He and security scoured every inch of the hotel, and scanned the video footage, though apparently she busted the camera in that hallway. My immediate thought was, *how convenient you little bitch*. They didn't find her, although we didn't come up empty handed. I threw her so hard she left a small blood stain behind, it got collected and sent in for analysis. In the cover of night she fled, but I would soon know who she was and I'd be ready. My devious mind schemed for her return.

Over the next few weeks, I assisted in planning my wedding and succumbed to being a public societal figure. In the past I worried about my transgressions slamming me in the face, but now I looked my fear in the eye and assisted in the hosting and planning of various charity events. I wanted this would-be assailant woman to find me. With my ears open and eyes peeled, I watched and waited.

Old Habits Die Hard

*S*am informed us he needed an indefinite hiatus to return to America. His mother fell ill, and the doctors didn't expect her to live much longer. I wished Sam the best as he departed. I'd miss him and his to-the-point personality but Sighed relief to be on my own again - freedom.

Early the morning after Sam left I glanced through the many hotel photo books looking for pictures of Didier's parents. I wanted to put together something special for him as a wedding gift. An hour into my search with a few fantastic pictures I spotted one of Didier and a young girl. Her pointy nose and witchy chin rang bells. Although she was much younger in the picture, I was positive it was the woman from the party. Didier knew her. I slipped the picture from the album sleeve to ask Jean, the concierge, if he remembered her.

If anybody did, it would be him. He'd been an employee at the hotel since Didier wore diapers.

Luckily for me, few customers were checking in and out so Jean wasn't busy. He greeted me with a warm smile and said in his deep French accent, "Bonne après midi madame."

"Good afternoon, Jean. I've been looking through pictures and I wanted your suggestions since you worked for Didier's parents."

"Oui, oui." He said as his lips curled upwards into a smile. I handed him the pictures, he looked through them, and carried on with a story behind each one. The final picture was of the young woman and Didier. He held it up to the light, in English with a heavy accent, said, "This is old. Her mother worked here in the kitchen and many a time she brought the girl, Halette or Halie as her mom often called her. Ah… she and Didier were good friends. She had a crush on him but then her family moved when her grandpa fell ill and they left to care for him. I think he would enjoy that picture."

"Do you remember her last name?"

He squinted his eyes upwards while furrows crossed his forehead. "So long ago... oui... Hardy, yes her father was an Englishman."

"Thanks for your help, Jean." I poured over my computer looking for a Halette Hardy. With a name that strange she couldn't be too difficult to find. After a couple searches I found her address.

The following day I packed my purse with a getaway costume, prettied myself up and used an ever popular female excuse. "I'm going shopping." Didier bought it and extended me a credit card.

The windows in her flat drawn open exposing the inside, I saw no movement. It had been a while since I "staked out" a residence. From a nearby café I watched while drinking coffee and reading. After thirty minutes of observing inactivity I snuck into her second floor flat in an older building.

While primping for "my shopping day" I tucked my hair into a beret using bobby pins. I pulled one out of my hair, slipped gloves over my hands, and picked at her door lock. When I heard the clicking sound I knew my lock-picking effort was successful.

I opened the door and stood before a sparsely furnished studio with a couple antiques and simple furniture. By the main living space window set a small round table with two reclining chairs and to the left, a kitchenette with two chairs on each side of a small rectangular block table. Papers piled inches above its surface. I dug through the pile underneath it and found a ticket to Aruba and pay stubs from a place called Mangeons. In her bedside dresser, buried in the bottom of her drawer I discovered a stack of letters written to Didier. I read through them and gagged at her drippy syrupy "I love you more than I can express" garbage. A blond wig lay beside her pile of love letters.

Footfalls in the hall outside her apartment alerted my attention then a jiggling sound of keys at the door left no room for doubt, I was no longer alone. Crap! I stole inside her closet and buried myself behind a huge coat. From slats in the closet, I saw her grabbing something from the top of her dresser. She didn't take off her shoes or set down her purse meaning her stay would be short, and I could leave in a few minutes. I stood motionless, not wanting to draw her attention my way, and waited. As soon as she turned the door knob to leave, her phone rang. She halted for a minute and talked then continued out the door. Whew! I wiped the sweat off my forehead. That had been a close call.

I allowed her enough time to leave the building, on a spontaneous notion I grabbed her blond wig and a ghostly crepe dress, and stuffed them into my bag. To spook her I used her lipstick to scribble over her letters to Didier, *It's you who doesn't belong*. Satisfaction welled up inside me as I marched out of her apartment wearing her blond wig.

I took the wig and dress with no clue how I'd use them; however, the refreshing walk home, and the familiar sight of street vagabonds allowed an idea to form inside my head, and a smile crept across my lips.

Payback's a Bitch

*H*alette claimed to manage a catering company but was in truth one of the cooks, not even the head chef! One of the ladies' charity groups I worked with was planning a banquet. I suggested Mangeons to cater, and she gave me the responsibility of booking. I called and made the arrangements, making sure that Halette was on the crew preparing and serving at the banquet.

Her DNA came back, and heralded nothing, no match in the system, which meant she had no arrests. But none of that mattered because I knew who she was, and her life was about to get a lot more complicated.

I found a transient, Gerty, who willingly took my money to wear Halette's wig and designer French clothing, a flowing cream dress made of crepe like material, while strutting across her path a few times. For a few nights I paid for a room in one of Paris' finest hotels and offered her a bulk of cash; I hoped she would use it wisely.

The night of the banquet, Gerty did a fabulous job and proved well worth the money. As Halette worked in the kitchen with the head chef preparing last minute food details Gerty strolled past her the first time. She walked past an open door leading from the kitchen, lingered in front of the door for just a moment before continuing, her back to Halette whose eyes followed Gerty. The second time Gerty passed, Halette carried a large serving tray. Gerty cocked her head downward as she almost floated past and Halette grew agitated and upset, her eyes expanded to the size of saucers and fear shot across her face. The final time Gerty passed, she lightly brushed past her from the backside. Halette immediately alerted to the touch and spun on her heels as Gerty walked out the kitchen door. She followed her out the door and down the street as if in a trance then Gerty disappeared as I paid her to do. The entire time, I made myself invisible as I didn't want Halette to notice me and ruin the fun.

I floated in and out of the guests before making my way to the security room with plates of food and drinks. The security guys were more than pleased with my generosity and loved my company. I watched the cameras while intriguing them with my feminine wiles until Gerty disappeared out the back. Halette followed her outside - my cue to finish what she started. There were no cameras outside so nobody would realize I was following her and I had a great alibi.

There was a chill in the air, and street lamps carried a soft warm glow above my head. Gerty disappeared from Halette's sight on a second story landing made of metal. Halette twisted and turned to find her, to no avail. She tiptoed towards the steps, as I dressed in the same garb as Gerty wore, made my way up the staircase towards her. "Hello, Halette, I'm so glad to meet you." I maintained a calm, cool voice.

She backed against the wall of the building and stammered, "How d... do... you know my n... name and why do you have m... my wig and dress?"

"You're the smart one. Who am I?"

She muttered under her breath and I responded, "I'm sorry I didn't hear that. Could you speak a tad bit louder?"

I edged closer my face illuminated and visible to her. "Justine, but you're not really. You're a fraud."

A sly smile twisted across my lips. "Then who am I?"

"I... I... don't know, but you're not Justine Holmes from Texas. Didier should be told."

I continued my glide up the steps. "Didier knows everything about me." That was a huge lie, but he didn't need to know more and there was so much about myself that I didn't understand. "Halie, can I call you that? Thanks." My voice a soothing almost-whisper. Beside her now, visible sweat beads formed on her forehead and her body tensed. My lips were within inches of her ear as I leaned towards her ear and whispered, "Stay out of my life."

She responded with actions instead of words pushing my body backwards. In an instant I fell in reverse and my fight or flight senses kicked on in self-defense. I grabbed hold of her as my body fell back and hit the metal grating behind me, she flew over the edge. I jumped up, looked towards the ground and spotted her limp body smashed against the pavement, blood pooling from her head. Butterflies of sorrow fluttered their wings inside me as I ran down the stairs and through the alley, barely glancing her way.

At a safe distance I stripped my undercover clothes away, along with the wig, and stuffed them inside a dumpster. Payphones in Paris took credit cards, which I considered under the circumstances would be foolish to use. That spoiled the entire anonymous thing. I wasn't going to use the cell Didier gave me, so I left her. Who was I kidding even if emergency calls could be made for free I wasn't about to incriminate myself. My conscience felt a slight tinge of guilt even though my actions were in self-defense. My prank brought her there and got her killed. I only meant to scare her.

With my morals getting the better of me, I sauntered back to the scene of the crime. If anyone asked I'd use the excuse I went for fresh air to cover up my discovery of her body. When I returned to Halette's body a car beat me to her parked beside the building, a man slung her into the trunk. I hid myself from his view and watched him close the trunk lid, get into the vehicle and drive away. Curiosity getting the better of me, I followed on foot until coming across a taxi.

"Where to?"

"Please follow that black sedan. The gentleman lost his wallet and I want to return it." I hoped I made my voice convincing. Either way, he continued on and followed Halette and her abductor.

The black sedan stopped near a bridge and I asked the cabby to let me out and circle back in twenty minutes, paying him double for the favor. Mist rose from the ground, creating a natural cover as I spied from a safe distance. The sedan driver dumped Halette's body into the river. The familiarity of his bulk forced me to edge closer through the surreal fog until I had a better view. He turned his head towards my direction, on impulse, I molded my body to the nearest tree. I was close enough to see his eyes bouncing in their sockets. Mr. Dancy Eyes! He followed me, but I didn't understand why he was covering up my crime. My own paranoia believed he meant to harm me. Then he drove off, leaving me in a quandary.

All Good Things Must Come to an End

A couple days after the Halette incident, and a few days before mine and Didier's wedding, my latest escapade still weighed on my mind like a load of gold bricks. My thoughts raced in circles. I couldn't stay, fearing Halettes' body turning up bringing negative publicity and hurting Didier. The event occurred near an affair I hosted. I took care to conceal my part in her death but I wasn't sure of my reaction when Halette's body hit the news. If I sweated even the tiniest bit Didier would discern it. In my past life I performed many questionable acts, but I never on purpose or by accident, killed another human being.

Mr. Dancy Eyes dumping her body into the river brought my past stinging front and center in my life, looming around my very presence. Not only the nightmares of her face that haunted my dreams but the mystery of my real parents and why someone would want a baby dead. Didier was wonderful, but he didn't know me. He knew Justine. His words, *Justine will you marry me?* Reverberated against the gray matter inside my head. It wouldn't be right to marry a man I hadn't been truthful with from the beginning? I loved being Justine and the woman at his side, but marriage? What if we had children? Would they be in danger and need personal bodyguards? Worse, they would have a fake mother!

I lived with a web of lies and deceit entangling me, which continued to twist around my soul. I didn't want to force that on anyone else - not my future children and not Didier. He meant more to me than entrapping him in my morbid life. People around me - the true me - died. I decided marrying him wasn't possible. His proposal ruined a good thing - correction I ruined a good thing when I flipped Halette over the railing. How would I tell him? The self-doubt

and shame bouncing in my head made me
aware I needed a plan.

My 24/7 bodyguards, Sam returned
soon after my shameful incident, and my
knight, Didier, compounded the ease of my
plan making things far more difficult. The
best chance for me to sneak out would be
through my terrace at night using darkness
as cover during Didier's absence from my
room. The terrace led across the top floor
of the hotel, an old, rickety set of service
stairs began at the end of the terrace
leading to an unused area. I figured for
safety I'd have to test them first.

I requested to hold the ceremony at
the hotel in all its grandiosity, which played
into my plan, and requested to Didier to be
alone the night before the wedding for
formality. It wasn't proper for the bride to
sleep with the groom the night before their
wedding. For our honeymoon, he was
planning something ornate, too bad I would
miss it. It was better I leave him now than
he discover my secrets later. It would hurt
him much less.

The day before our wedding, I stayed in
my room. People came in and out with last
minute alterations and changes, but mostly
I was alone. My white wedding dress looked

like something belonging to Cinderella or Snow White and accentuated my curves. My body developed so much in the past couple of years I no longer looked sickly, waif-ish, or childish, but an eighteen year old full grown woman. Didier believed me to be twenty.

With the wedding preparations finished and the hotel wedding hustle slowed, I organized myself for departure checking my backpack to make sure the items I came with were present. I was leaving with nothing more than I came, except the clothes on my back and the memories in my head. I wouldn't forget Didier or his kindness towards me. I loved him, one day I'd be back. My heart ached with my choice of leaving but I saw no other alternative. My past came to the forefront of my life, to move forward I needed to move backwards and find the answers to my mysteries. To put my soul at ease and put an end to my hiding and fears I needed to find the answers to my cryptic birth and biological parents. I sat with paper and pen, but no words to say, nothing described the roller coaster my emotions were riding or why I was leaving. After several minutes of staring at the paper, I wrote...

I love you. I'm sorry. Don't forget me ever. I will never forget you.
  Justine

With a heavy flow of tears pouring from my eyes I tucked each corner of my sheets underneath the mattress and smoothed the comforter so no wrinkles showed than placed my note on the edge of the bed. I pulled my hair into a floppy hat, grabbed my backpack and opened the terrace door without a squeak. Darkness had fallen, but the moon and stars cast a glow lighting my path as I gingerly walked across the terrace, through the gate, and towards the stairs.

Every creak sounded like a siren. I feared each step on the rickety old stairs would send them and me tumbling to the ground. Halfway down the stairs swayed, my pulse quickened, and I grabbed for the railing and held on edging slow - one precious step at a time. When I placed my first foot on the asphalt it felt wonderful beneath my feet. I rested my back against the building for a few seconds, observed my surroundings while my pulse resumed its normal pace. I overheard the staff talking close by, so I waited.

After many minutes, I heard footsteps pound off in the opposite direction. I edged closer to where they stood and peaked my head around the corner. The area was empty. With my backpack firmly on my shoulders I glided past the hotel to the street and walked for a few blocks, holding my head low.

Once I was far enough from the hotel I hailed a taxi and asked the driver take me to the airport. On the ride, I thought about Didier waking up in the morning. I wouldn't be there. He wouldn't know this at first; not until his staff told him when there was no answer from my room. The staff would come in using their key and I would be gone. I'm sure he would use financial resources to try and find me, but I'd again change my identity and appearance. Justine Holmes would be no more.

Happy Trails...

Moonlighting in Paris

Answers

y challenge of the day was moving through Paris undetected. I rolled my hair into a bun and wore a floppy dark green hat with a short brim over it. To further my disguise, I considered wearing heavy makeup, using bold chunks of color, but feared it would bring too much unwanted attention. I needed to blend, not stand out, so I settled for no makeup. I arrived at the airport and boarded the plane without one paparazzo chasing after me and snapping pictures. Security had been an ordeal when I showed the security agent my ID - he asked for an autograph. I leaned towards him and asked him to keep it quiet, then I signed my John Hancock, or rather Justine's. On the second flight into the U.S. a fellow passenger of male persuasion shouted, "Hey, you're Justine Holmes." Thank my goodies most passengers were sleeping.

I looked him square in the eye and said, "Nope, but thank you for the comparison."

Baffled, he scrunched his brows and pinched his lips. I ignored him and he went away. The next forty-eight hours I attempted to stay hidden, with a book in front of my face, in the most vacated areas of the airport.

I purchased a last-minute flight taking me from Paris to Berlin then to Chicago. When I landed in Chicago, I wasted no time in changing my appearance and identity. I stopped at a twenty-four-hour drug store and purchased blond hair coloring and strange glasses. The glasses had thin round gold frames with tinted lenses to dull my eye color. They looked like reading glasses, but the lenses lacked magnification.

I checked into a low budget motel using cash under an assumed name. I didn't want to leave a trail. In my room I pulled an old pair of scissors I found during my dumpster diving days out of my backpack and cut my hair, which reached to my waist. After I finished chopping, it reached to the bottom of my neck, just above my shoulders. I brushed out my hair and turned my head upside down to cut leaving it with short layers. Next, I bleached it turning it an orangey yellow. I didn't look like Justine anymore. Mission accomplished.

I sat on my bed plotting out my next move and contacted my friend James, hoping to gain yet another ID, and catch up on his and LulaBell's lives. Luckily, he still lived in the motel, hiding out, using code I explained what I needed, he seemed to understand. "Got it! See you in a few days sweetie."

I planned on paying him generously for his assistance. Happy with my appearance, I left. The next few days I spent weaving around the country on busses until I reached my location. It was strange being back where I lost my love Einstein. Fear and sadness welled up in my belly, but I needed to do this.

I knocked on James' door, he opened it wide, placed his large hands on my shoulders and widened his eyes scanning me head to toe with intensity. "Wow! You have changed. I saw your picture on a magazine one day and I thought, 'I know that girl'. You're stunning even with that tangerine hair."

"It looks like a straw mop, but I don't look like the girl on that magazine, do I?"

"No, you do not!" He maneuvered his head back and forth as if to emphasis *No*. I followed him inside the room. "Justine's disappearance is going to break many a young man's heart," he said with a softness in his eyes. The crow's feet around them deeper and a few more wrinkles graced his forehead, but he still looked like James. He was the only person alive who understood anything about my woes.

"They will have to miss her. Where is LulaBell?"

"She is taking classes at the junior college. She should be home within the hour."

"College? She is only a couple years younger than me, but I can't imagine her as old enough to of graduated."

"Dual enrollment, high school classes along with college classes."

We spent the next couple hours waiting for LulaBell, catching up on our lives. I relayed my entire experience in Paris. How Halette stalked me and the nasty trick I played that started with a confrontation between her and I ending with her flipping over the railing, being carried off and thrown into a river by Mr. Dancy Eyes. I told him about Didier and leaving him at the altar because I was afraid the police would find Halette's body and trace it back to me which was partly true. I figured if I couldn't trust the man who made me a new ID every time I called, who could I trust? With all I confided in him, somehow, I still refused to discuss my search for the truth behind my birth and "kidnapping". The words in my mom's letter, Don't *ever let them find ya. They won't hestate to kill ya*, pounded in my head forcing my brain to resist any efforts to seek another soul's help in my search. However, he proved a good, confidential friend, and I needed to get most of the craziness and secrecy off my chest. He listened as I poured out my heart, once again I cried in his comforting arms. He said that Einstein's death was a big thing.

After I finished my crying bout, he handed me a beer, and we sat in the courtyard like old times. "It almost seems as though I never left," I said, sitting across the table from him and feeling as though Einstein would at any moment walk up and plop in the seat beside me, planting a kiss upon my cheek.

"Those were good times we had. Do you still cook?"

"I haven't much. There was no need Didier gave me everything. I miss it."

"You were some cook." His voice reminded me of the best time in my life when Einstein and I made a life together. "I don't want to bring up sad times for you, but how much did you learn of Einstein's death?"

"Only what I found online through papers. As much as it hurts, I want to know more."

"His family's wealthy, rich people's runaway children don't turn up dead every day. When Einstein disappeared, he was fifteen, at first the police suggested kidnapping, but no ransom request or any contact from the 'would be' kidnappers appeared. Their next possible scenario was abduction by a random pervert or killed and his body dumped. But his body never turned up anywhere. The police even suspected his parent's, but with no body there was nothing for them to pursue. Last they deduced he ran away. His parents' money and contacts made it impossible for the police and newspaper gossips to discover why."

I realized from personal experience now that money bought almost anything, even steel walls. "I am curious myself why Einstein ran away. He must've had everything. Why leave it?" I paused contemplating my words for a moment. "I had everything, and I ran away too. Money can buy a lot, but not happiness. I ran because I was in trouble, fear of a commitment to a man who really didn't know me... I told myself it wasn't fair to him. Maybe Einstein had been in trouble - something that money couldn't fix. It makes sense how he moved through homes like a ghost, understood the basics of alarms, and robbed the homeowners' blind."

James changed the flow of the conversation. "It seems you lived a privileged life in Paris."

"Yeah... I'm exhausted and turning in for the night, tell LulaBell we'll catch up later."

"Will do, night Cleo."

I paid cash up front for three days, figuring it would take at least that for my new ID to arrive. Every room looked similar and everything reminded me of Einstein, from the cheesy bed cover with vines patterned across it to the curtains. I flash-backed to the night we arrived here several years ago, how happy we both were with the simplicity of taking a hot shower. After years of living on the streets, jumping cities, stealing anything we could find of value and running innocentish scams on people to pickpocket their wallets, a hot shower and warm bed felt like a dream that night. My eyes filled with tears, I buried my head in a pillow crying myself to sleep.

The following day I contemplated everything I learned and considered what I still needed to learn compiling a short list. My mom was obviously not my real mom, but I needed to understand who she was to find my biological family - who she was hiding from, and why Slug wanted to kill a baby? To move forward I needed to work backwards. It seemed that's always what made sense.

1. find out about mom/ follow every lead

2. find real family/ be cautious

3. find out who wanted me dead/ be extremely cautious

4. Why did Einstein run?

My first order of business was to buy a cell phone equipped with internet and GPS with a pay-as-you-go plan. After doing so I found an internet coffee house. The unknown assailant murdered my mom at age thirty-five, which made her twenty-three when she acquired me. She wasn't in with good people, she had survival skills and street smarts, but no formal education judging by her childlike spelling and penmanship. I deduced she ran away from home.

Hundreds, thousands of children went missing daily, no shocker to me as I had fit that category myself. I didn't know where she lived as a child. I searched and searched missing children assuming my mom ran away between the ages of thirteen to sixteen, scanning the three-year window state to state.

Nothing. Nothing fitting my mom; although I found strange, disturbing stories. In North Carolina I read about the discovery of a young woman who took a nasty spill down a mountain. Her clothing torn to shreds and her face, hands and legs bruised and bleeding. She lay in a hospital bed in a catatonic state. The police believed she witnessed a brutal murder across the street from her home. Although intriguing the story had nothing to do with my search. I clicked off the page getting back on track. The coffee house was closing. In the morning I'd get up early and visit the public library.

At the library the next day, I again searched like a hound dog chasing a fox.

My eyes went buggy from reading the computer screen, then something caught my eye. A young girl, fifteen, went missing at approximately the same year my mom would have turned fifteen. There was a picture, and the girl looked like a young version of my mom - freckles, long light hair, dark eyes, approximate weight 95 lbs., a height of five feet. Her name was Perdita Ferguson and her parents were Thane and Leila Ferguson. I pulled my tablet with questions out of my backpack, scribbled the information onto a blank paper inside and continued searching, looking for an address. I found one in Georgia. Her parent's strange names made address finding possible, had they been Jane or John Smith' I'd never found them.

After three days, James produced my new identity. LulaBell, now a stunning, shapely young woman, and James transported me to the local bus station. My ID said I was twenty-one-year-old Shanna Nu. As I stepped out of the car, I slipped him an envelope with a wad of cash. "It's time for me to leave again. Thank you so much for your help and making me of legal drinking age." I gave him a huge bear hug.

The corners of his mouth turned upwards at the ends in a smile. "No problem, you find those answers. If you need help again, you know where to find me."

LulaBell stepped out of the truck, wrapped her arms around me and whispered, "Be careful, Cleo."

I wasn't sure how much she understood about her father's illegal dealings, although she wasn't a young child anymore, I imagined she understood quite a bit. I entered the station catching the next bus to Allentown, Georgia.

LulaBell's words stuck with me during the ride. *Be careful Cleo.* If only she knew the half of it. I had money from my nest egg, and self-defense skills that already paid off in Paris. Armed for battle and ready to uncover the secrets to my existence I plotted my moves. How would I approach Mr. and Mrs. Ferguson? I couldn't walk up to the Fergusons' door and tell them about their missing child/child abductor/junkie/murdered daughter. This situation must be approached with care, maybe I'd stake-out their home for a couple days. That's it! I had a kid's play police badge from my dumpster diving days, but it looked real at a quick glance. I'd pretend to be a detective and with respect pick their brains. With that in mind, I got off at the next stop, bought a navy-blue women's suit, a white blouse, along with conservative heels and a flip pad and blue pen. I'd wrap my hair into a bun going heavy on the makeup to appear older.

Jaw Dropper

*U*pon arrival in Dublin, Georgia - Allentown sat outside the city limits - the sun set as dusk settled. I checked into a motel for the night, stiff from the bus ride I perused the small city. My stomach gurgled nasty words, so I stopped at a bar and grill for dinner. As I ate, I reflected on how good it felt to be back in the States. In Paris I forgot how much I loved the U.S. and how vast its borders are, causing the perception I was looking for a needle in a haystack.

A young man uninvited, sat in the booth across from me and introduced himself, "Hi, I'm Bub Richards." He extended his hand in greeting. I didn't extend mine back. It floored me how he plopped into the booth like I invited him. He had soft blue eyes, chestnut wavy hair and a baby face - not too shabby to look at, but he had an awful lot of gall.

"I'm leaving, nice to meet you, Bub." I said standing up to leave.

"You're a dazzling beautiful woman and I couldn't help myself. I'm sorry." A poor try to remediate his failed attempt.

"Like I said, I'm leaving." I slipped money to the server and walked out the door.

No sooner did I walk out the door than I heard footsteps behind me. Fear surfaced inside me as the terrors of my past came rushing back. I slipped around the corner and waited. Soon enough, a form drew closer as I watched its shadow through the streetlights glide across the pavement. I positioned myself and brought my leg out in front of me as the shadow person walked past my spot. This caused him to trip and fall flat on his face. Familiar tufts of chestnut hair crashed forward.

"Bub? Oh, I'm so sorry. I thought maybe... nevermind. Why are you following me?" I offered my hand to help him up from the pavement. His nose was bloody. My self-defense skills affected people that way, I reflected, remembering when I threw Halette over my shoulder in Paris, twice.

He took my hand and sheepishly said, "I just think you're beautiful and wanted to know you better." Ay yi yi, what was it with men?

"OK, your nose is bleeding. I'll buy you a drink." A small pang of guilt crept into my soul.

His face lit up and a huge smile creased his lips as blood trickled down his chin in a slow but steady stream. "That'd be nice."

I bought him a drink while the bartender readied a rag and ice for his nose. "It might be broken." Pangs of guilt shot through my soul.

The bartender, a young dark-haired woman with surreal emerald eyes, chuckled. "He'll be okay. At least once a week he incurs the wrath of one young lady or another."

"So, you're a lady chaser and I was on the menu for tonight?"

His face turned as red as a tomato. "Can't we enjoy this drink before you run off again?" He stared into my eyes with ferocity, it made me uncomfortable. Then he drew closer. "You look a lot like that model. The one who's dating the really rich French guy, umm Jennifer... no Juniper... I got it" As if he found the pot of gold at the end of the rainbow he shouted, "Justine!"

Was it ever going to end? Would I always be Justine to people? "Sure, yup, that's me." His eyes grew wide and his mouth dropped from its jaw, I thought I would have to catch it and glue it back on his face. "I'm joking, allow me to introduce myself, since I bloodied your nose, I suppose it's the least I can do. I'm Shanna."

He picked his jaw off the ground. "Nice to meet you, Shanna. You aren't from here, cause I know everyone and no one beautiful as you lives anywhere near here. So, you visiting?"

Gees, were his syrupy pick-up lines ever going to stop? "No, more like business." I used my best cop voice as practice before meeting the "grandparents" tomorrow and picked his brain since he claimed he *knew* everyone.

"Have you met Thane and Leila Ferguson?"

"Oh yeah, Thane was a mean S.O.B. when he drank liquor. Heart disease killed him, maybe it was something else, but he's dead. Leila is a sweet lady, real quiet, always home." A mean drunk father, no wonder my mom ran.

Bub and I enjoyed several drinks before he insisted on giving me his number and attempting to go back to my cheap motel room with me. I gave him a peck on the cheek and told him good night. He

would never be aware that he met the
famous Justine Holmes.

Moonlighting in Paris